KAY THOMPSON'S

ELOISE

THE ABSOLUTELY ESSENTIAL
60th Anniversary Edition

Drawings by
HILARY KNIGHT

INCLUDING
the original *ELOISE*
and the full-color Eloise scrapbook
with rare photos & drawings
from the files of Hilary Knight

SCRAPBOOK WRITTEN BY
MARIE BRENNER

AND COLORFUL COMMENTS BY
ME, ELOISE

Simon & Schuster Books for Young Readers
New York London Toronto Sydney New Delhi

KAY THOMPSON'S

ELOISE

DRAWINGS BY
HILARY KNIGHT

A BOOK FOR PRECOCIOUS GROWN-UPS

SIMON & SCHUSTER BOOKS FOR YOUNG READERS
AN IMPRINT OF SIMON & SCHUSTER
CHILDREN'S PUBLISHING DIVISION
1230 AVENUE OF THE AMERICAS,
NEW YORK, NEW YORK 10020
COPYRIGHT © 1955 BY KAY THOMPSON
COPYRIGHT RENEWED 1983 BY KAY THOMPSON
SCRAPBOOK TEXT COPYRIGHT © 1999 BY MARIE BRENNER.
PORTIONS OF THE SCRAPBOOK TEXT HAVE APPEARED IN *VANITY FAIR*.
IMAGES OF ELOISE, INCLUDING THOSE ON PAGE 79, AND RELATED MATERIALS,
DRAWN BY HILARY KNIGHT, COPYRIGHT © 1955, 1999 BY THE ESTATE OF KAY THOMPSON.
PHOTO OF KAY THOMPSON PAGE 71 (CREDIT: ARTHUR ERMATES) USED BY PERMISSION
OF CULVER PICTURES. PHOTOS PAGE 68, 73 (GARLAND), 74, 80 (CREDIT: MARK FERRI), 83;
LITHOGRAPH BY DON FREEMAN PAGE 75; ALL IMAGES PAGE 77 (OTHER THAN MAGAZINE COVER)
FROM THE COLLECTION OF HILARY KNIGHT. ILLUSTRATIONS OF KAY THOMPSON ET AL. PAGES 73, 74, 75,
AND ILLUSTRATIONS PAGE 78, 79 COPYRIGHT © 1999 BY HILARY KNIGHT. ADVERTISEMENT PAGE 70 USED
BY PERMISSION OF THE PLAZA HOTEL. MAGAZINE PHOTOGRAPH PAGE 71 USED BY PERMISSION OF
GOOD HOUSEKEEPING. PHOTOS PAGES 72, 73 (FREED UNIT AND GARLAND/MINNELLI) USED BY
PERMISSION OF PHOTOFEST. PHOTO OF LENA HORNE PAGE 73 USED BY PERMISSION OF NATIONAL
FILM ARCHIVE. *THE NEW YORKER* COVER PAGE 77 REPRINTED BY PERMISSION; © 1926
(RENEWED 1954, 1992); ORIGINALLY IN *THE NEW YORKER*; ALL RIGHTS RESERVED.
ALL RIGHTS RESERVED, INCLUDING THE RIGHT OF REPRODUCTION IN WHOLE
OR IN PART IN ANY FORM. SIMON & SCHUSTER BOOKS FOR YOUNG READERS IS A
TRADEMARK OF SIMON & SCHUSTER, INC. "ELOISE" AND RELATED MARKS ARE TRADEMARKS
OF THE ESTATE OF KAY THOMPSON. FOR INFORMATION ABOUT SPECIAL DISCOUNTS FOR
BULK PURCHASES, PLEASE CONTACT SIMON & SCHUSTER SPECIAL SALES AT 1-866-506-1949 OR
BUSINESS@SIMONANDSCHUSTER.COM. THE SIMON & SCHUSTER SPEAKERS BUREAU CAN
BRING AUTHORS TO YOUR LIVE EVENT. FOR MORE INFORMATION OR TO BOOK AN
EVENT, CONTACT THE SIMON & SCHUSTER SPEAKERS BUREAU AT 1-866-248-3049
OR VISIT OUR WEBSITE AT WWW.SIMONSPEAKERS.COM.
BOOK DESIGN BY EINAV AVIRAM
MANUFACTURED IN CHINA / 0815 SCP
2 4 6 8 10 9 7 5 3 1
CIP DATA FOR A PREVIOUS EDITION OF THIS BOOK IS
AVAILABLE AT THE LIBRARY OF CONGRESS.
ISBN 978-1-4814-5706-4
ISBN 978-1-4814-5707-1 (EBOOK)

I am Eloise

I am six

I am a city child
I live at The Plaza

8

There is a lobby which is enormously large
with marble pillars and ladies in it and a revolving
door with 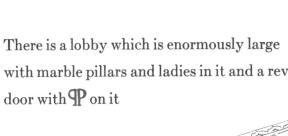 on it

I spend an awful lot of time in the lobby
For instance every day I have to go to the
Desk Clerk and see what's happening there

Then I stop by the Mail Desk to see if they have any stamps

Then I go to the House Phones
and make several calls to see
if anybody's in

The Bell Captain knows who I am

If there is a lot of luggage trying to get in the elevator
and these people are all in a crowd and smoking and from
out of town or something, I edge into the middle of it and
lose my skate key

I am a nuisance in the lobby
Mr. Salomone said so
He is the Manager
I always say "Good morning, Mr. Salomone"
and he always says "Good morning, Eloise"

My mother knows The Owner

I live on the top floor

Of course I am apt to be on any floor at any time

And if I want to go anywhere I simply take the elevator

For instance if I happen to be on the second floor I just

press that button until it comes up and as soon as that

door is open I get in and say "*5th floor* please" and

when those doors clank shut we ride up and I get out on

the *5th floor* and as soon as that elevator is out of

sight I skibble up those stairs to the *8th floor* and then

I press that button and when that same elevator comes up and

as soon as that door is open I get in and say "*15th floor*

please" and then when those doors clank shut we ride up

and I get out on the *15th floor* and as soon as that elevator

is out of sight I skibble down to the *12th floor* and press

that button and when that same elevator comes up and those

doors open I say "*The Lobby* please" and then those doors

clank shut and we ride down without saying absolutely one word

and then I get into the next elevator and go all the way up.

Then I get off at the top floor

And look in the mirror at me

END
HERE

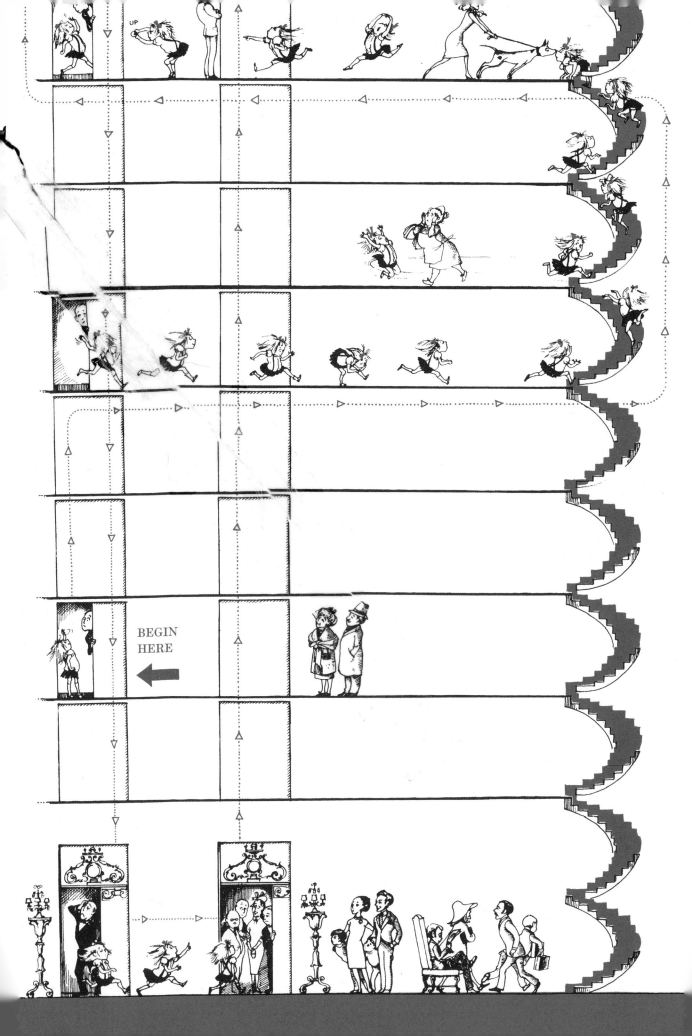

UP

BEGIN
HERE
←

ve down at the end of the hall

metimes I take two sticks and skidder them along the walls

d when I run down the hall I slomp my feet against the

odwork which is very good for scuffing and noise

metimes I slomp my skates if I want to make a really loud

d terrible racket

We have a buzzer on our front door

I always lean on it

That's how Nanny knows it's me

ELOISE

Nanny is my nurse
She wears tissue paper in her dress
and you can hear it
She is English and has 8 hairpins
made out of bones
She says that's all she needs in
this life for Lord's sake

Nanny says she would rawther I didn't
talk talk talk all the time
She always says everything 3 times
like Eloise you cawn't cawn't cawn't
Sometimes I hit her on the ankle with a tassel
She is my mostly companion

19

I have my own room

It has a coat rack which is as large as me

I have a dog that looks like a cat

His name is Weenie

Sometimes I put sunglasses on him

Then I have to scratch his back with a wire hanger

I have a turtle

His name is Skipperdee

He eats raisins and wears sneakers

The Plaza is the only hotel in New York

that will allow you to have a turtle

Skipperdee and me we always know its morning
because Weenie breathes in our face and kisses us

The absolutely first thing I have to do
is braid Skipperdee's ears
Otherwise he gets cross and develops a rash

Nanny gets up feeling tired tired tired
and puts on her kimono
and skibbles over to slam those windows
down shut so that we don't
freeze freeze freeze

Then she stretches her muscles
and feels fresh fresh fresh

Nanny yawns out loud

Then I pick up the telephone
and call Room Service

Oooooooooo I absolutely love Room Service
They always know its me
and they say "Yes, Eloise?"
And I always say "Hello, this is me ELOISE and would you
kindly send one roast-beef bone, one raisin and seven spoons
to the top floor and charge it please
Thank you very much"

Then I hang up and look at the ceiling
for a while and think of a
way to get a present

I usually yawn out loud several times

Then Nanny gives the signal and Weenie and Skipperdee and me

we skibble out of bed as fast as everly we can and Nanny wraps

us in our robe and holds us tight

And I pat her on her botto

which is large

Then we have to do our morning duties and laugh and sing

London from bottom to top is zup

The keeper in the shop is zup

And even Mrs. Mop is zup

Oh what a love-a-ly mawning

In Trafalgar Square the Bobby's zup

In Piccadilly the Nippy's zup

In Covent Garden the Clippy's zup

Oh what a love-a-ly mawning

We're zup and we've got to be jolly clean

From head to toe and in between

Zup good morning and how've ya been

Oh what a love-a-ly mawning

The Royal Navy is up-is-zup

Buckingham Palace is up-is-zup

And even the BBC is-zup

Oh what a love-a-ly

Oh what a love-a-ly

Oh what a love-a-ly mawning

The Roy-al Na-vy is up-is-zup   Buck-ing-ham Pal-ace is

up-is-zup And e-ven the B B C is-zup   Oh what a love-a-ly

Oh what a   love-a-ly   Oh what a   love-a-ly   maw – ning

26

Ooooooooo I just love Nanny I absolutely do

While I'm brushing my teeth there is this pigeon who is always
hanging around our bathroom window and he does absolutely nothing
but coo
He is fat and grisly and I holler at him and he
flies over to the Sherry-Netherland for a while to see what they're
up to

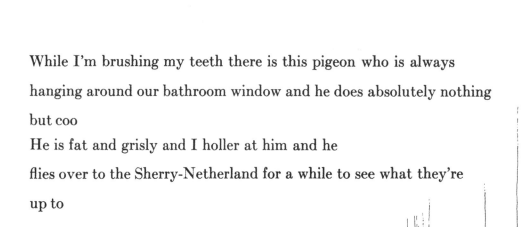

Weenie and me weigh 36
Nanny weighs 18 stones

Skipperdee weighs absolutely nothing at all
unless he has his sneakers on
Then of course he weighs ½

Then Nanny puts on her corset which is

Kleenex makes a very good hat

When we are clean we skibble in our scuffs to the kitchen

and there is René with Room Service

René always says "Bonjour, Eloise, voici votre petit déjeuner"

Nanny always says "My my my doesn't that look good!"

And I always say "Bonjour, René, merci and charge it please

Nanny has Irish bacon
which reminds her of her brother

You have to eat oatmeal or you'll dry up
Anybody knows that

Nanny likes her coffee hot hot hot
An egg cup makes a very good hat

31

I have two dolls which is enough

Their names are Sabine and Saylor

Sabine is a rag doll and she has absolutely no face at all

partially because she came from Jamaica by Air Express

Otherwise she has shoe-button eyes and two right legs

She is *rawther* unusual

Saylor is a very large doll and has a hard head and no arms

She was in the most terriblest accident and she bleeded so hard

she almost choked in the night and this ambulance came and took

her to this hospital and it was an emergency and they had to give

her all this terribly dark medicine and a lot of Band-aids and when

she came back home she was weak weak weak and had to take cod-liver

oil

I gave her a strawberry leaf from under my grapefruit for not

whimpering and Weenie licked her face

They have to have a teaspoon of water every hour or so, so you can

see they are an extremely lot of extra work

HOSPITAL

X-RAY

Here's what I like to do

Make things up

Here's what I can do

Chew gum

Write

Spell

Stand on my head for the longest amount of time

34

Stand on my toes

Get dizzy and fall down

Make a terrible face

nd here's the thing of it

ost of the time I'm on the telephone

35

My day is rawther full

I have to call the Valet and tell him

to get up here and pick up

my sneakers to be cleaned and pressed

and have them back for

sure without fail

Then I have to play the piano

and look in the mirror for a while

Then I have to open and close the door for a while and as

soon as I hear talking and laughing I skidder out and run down

the hall

and if there is an open door I have

to walk in and pretend I am an orphan

and sometimes I limp and sort of bend

to the side and look sort of

sad in between the arms

and they give me a piece of melon or something

Then I roam around the halls

Then I have to scurry down to
the 10th floor to adjust those
thermostats in case anyone needs it

If there's a fire on the 6th floor
I know how to fix it

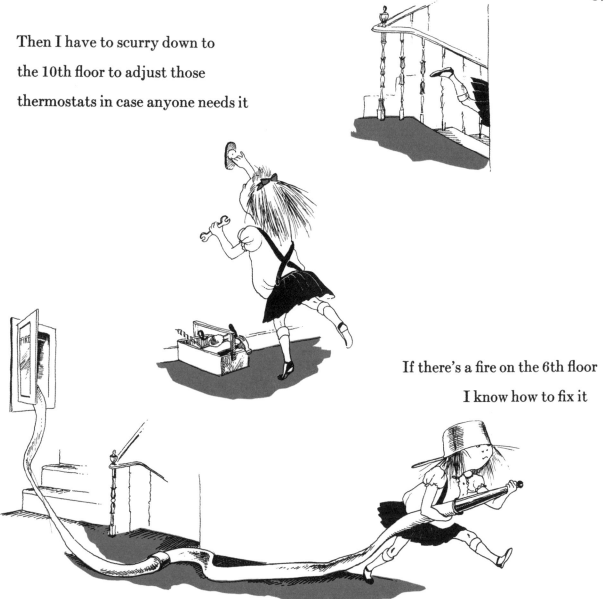

Then I have to hide and see what those Hotel Officers are up to

All they do is walk and talk

I have never been arrested

Then I have to hurry back to the top floor

Our day maid's name is Johanna

She has earrings with garnets

and is going to take her Social Security

to Bavaria on her birthday

One time she saw this man in this hair net

and he bawled her out for taking his razor blades

I have to help her put on those

pillowcases or she'll never be through

by 4 for Lord's sake

She has to be through by 4

Then I have to go around to that Service Elevator on the 6th floor
and see what everybody's thrown away and if I want it or not, like
ribbon or something like that

Then I have to go down to help the Switchboard Operator
in case there are any D As and there has to be
some sort of message taken or something like that

If there is an Exit sign I always have to go into it because there might be a mattress in there and I can lie down on it and get some rest so I can carry on for Lord's sake

Oh my Lord I am absolutely so busy I don't know how I can possibly get everything done

Then I have to hop around for a while

I have lunch at the Palm Court if it is too rainy

and see Thomas

We are both rawther fond of talking and he gives

me Gugelhopfen

Thomas has a son in the Marines who got married

on a shoestring

Thomas has a Corvette

always go in the Persian Room after 4 to see my friend Bill

He is a busboy in the night and goes to school in the day and

his eyes water

Here's where he's been

Madrid

Here's where I've been

Boiler Room

Then I scamper to the Terrace Room

where those debutantes are prancing around

Then I have to skibble into the Baroque Room because sometimes there is this chalk and there is this pitcher with ice water in it and you should see the cigar smoke left over from a General Motors meeting Oh my Lord

Then I have to help the busboys and waiters get set up in the
Crystal Room
They always wait until the last second for Lord's sake and then
we have to rush our feet off

I go to all the weddings in the White and Gold Room

and I usually stay for the reception

There are absolutely nothing but rooms in The Plaza

Oooooooooooooooooo I absolutely love The Plaza

Sometimes if they are having this enormous affair
in the Grand Ballroom I get there early to help Joe
set up the lights in the ceiling and before anybody gets
there we just scamper up this ladder and hide up there
in those holes

Oh my Lord is it ever swelteringly hot up there

I always wear my sun visor

I am all over the hotel

Half the time I am lost

But mostly I am on the first floor because

that's where Catering is

So I have to go down there every day for at least

three hours and sometimes I have to go at night

Oh my Lord do they ever have a lot of things going on

down there

Altogether I have been to 56 affairs including Halloween

There is this Oak Room which is to the right if you want to have

a broken mint or something like that

And you have to go downstairs
to the Rendezvous Room which is
very good for hiding over a long
period of time and for doing
a tour jeté or so

The Package Room has all these packages in it and sometimes
I have to help them lift those heavy boxes and look for small
packages that might be for me ELOISE

metimes I go into the Men's Room which is very good for playing

ailroad Station or something like that

Every Wednesday I have to go to the Barber Shop
and have Vincent shape my hair
He does absolutely nothing but talk and swiggles
me around in that chair and hurts my neck with
that whiskbroom

Sometimes I sklonk him in the kneecap

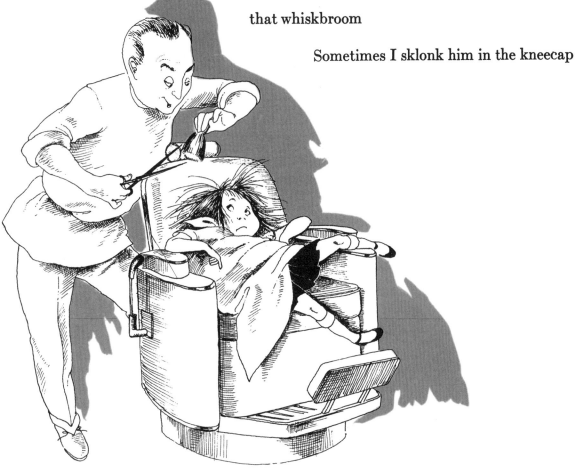

Vincent says that if I am not careful I am not going

to have a hair on my head by the time I'm 7 for Lord's sake

Getting bored is not allowed

Sometimes I comb my hair with a fork

Sometimes I wear my arm in a sling

Sometimes I put a rubber band

on the end of my nose

Toe shoes make very good ears

Sometimes I wear them to lunch

Here's what I like to do

Pretend

Sometimes I am a mother with 40 children

Sometimes I am a giant with fire coming out of my hair

Sometimes I get terribly sick and have to be waited on

Sometimes I get so sick my head falls over and is wobbling until

it is loose

Then we have to call my mother long distance and charge it

My mother is 30 and has a charge account at Bergdorf's

She wears a 3½ shoe

I put a large cabbage leaf on my head

when I have a headache

It makes a very good hat

My mother knows Coco Chanel

50

goes to Europe and to Paris

sends for me if there's some sun

always packed in case I have to leave on TWA

moment's notice or something like that

mother has A T & T stock and she knows an ad man

tever that is

Sometimes my mother goes to Virginia

with her lawyer

He has an office on Madison Avenue

He has already had the whooping

cough and the measles

Sometimes I give him rubber candy

He is absolutely so dumb he eats it

Sometimes he brings me a present

whether I deserve it or not

I usually do

Here's what he likes

Martinis

Here's what I like

Dandelions

But not very often

I absolutely dislike school

so Philip is my tutor

He goes to Andover

My mother knows the Dean

He wears red garters and is boring boring boring

When we have our French lesson he reads in French about la petite
cousine de Marie and her jardin and sometimes I listen to him but
not very often

Here's what makes Philip angry

He says "Alors! nous commençerons" and I say "Alors! nous commencerons"

And he says "Shall we settle down Eloise? And I say "Shall we settle down Eloise?"

And he says "That's quite enough Eloise"

And I say "That's quite enough Eloise"

And he says "I mean it Eloise"

And I say "I mean it Eloise" right back at him

And he looks at me with fiercely eyes

And I look right back at him with fiercely eyes

And then he says "That will do Eloise"

And then I say "That will do Eloise"

And then he shouts "Eloise I mean it"

And then I shout "Eloise I mean it" right after him

And then he gets madder and says "Stop it at once Eloise"

And then I say "Stop it at once Eloise"

And then he stands up and says "Very well Eloise"

And then I stand up and say "Very well Eloise"

And then he walks around the room

And then I walk around the room

And then he screams "Nanny"

Then I scream "Nanny"

And Nanny comes in yelling "Non non non Eloise" and she claps her hands and Skipperdee and me we skibble over and hide behind the television or fall dead behind a hidden door

And then Nanny puts her arm around Philip and calls Room Service and says "Send three of everything please"

And when the waiter brings the check Nanny signs my mother's name

And I simply tell him to "charge it please and thank you very much"

> Then I do a cartwheel

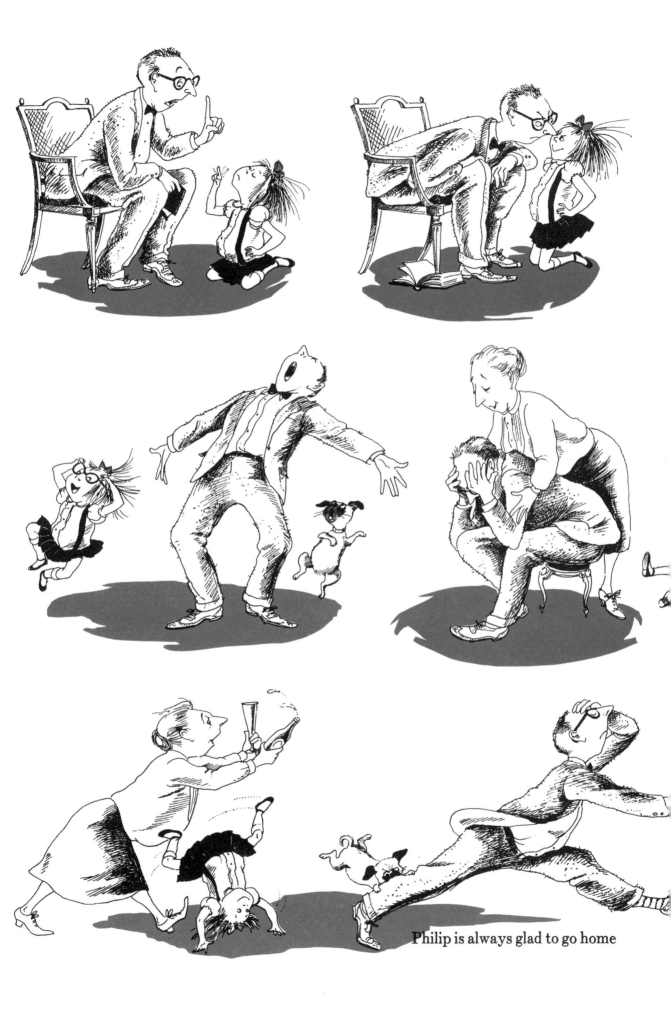

Philip is always glad to go home

Every night I have to call Room Service to send up that menu

so we can order our dinner for Lord's sake

I always have to read it for a few seconds or so

Then I just say "I'll have the Planked Medallion of Beef Tenderloin

with Fresh Vegetables Maison please and two raisins, one strawberry

leaf and one clams in season s'il vous plaît and charge it please

Thank you very much"

Ooooooooooooooooo I absolutely love Room Service

The night maid's name is Lily

She married the engineer of the subway and cut her hair

but I think she's sorry

She gives us extra pillowcases and soap

Once there was this most terriblest storm that came up and

it rained and all this thunder was clomping itself into

this water and all these people were drowning without air

Absolutely no one was saved

Paper cups are very good for talking to Mars

TV is in the Drawing Room

I always watch it with my parasol in case there's some sort of glare

And oh my Lord when it's fight night Nanny is absolutely wild and we

have to scamper into our places and get ready and Nanny has to find

her Players and I have to get my binoculars and call Room Service

and order three Pilsener Beers for Nanny and one meringue glacée

for me ELOISE and charge it please

Thank you very much

Here's what I hate

Howdy Doody

Oooooooooooooooooooo I absolutely love TV

Every night when it's time to go to bed Nanny yawns out loud

and says she is tired tired tired

I make as much noise as I possibly can like turning on the phonograph

real loud and hollering a lot

Then I have to brush Nanny's hair

for her

And then we both yawn out loud and

get into our pajamas

Then I have to put on my Don't Disturb sign and get Skipperdee and

Weenie and me all tucked in and then Nanny opens the windows

enormously wide so we can have air air air

Then she turns out the light

Nanny has a mole   61

Sometimes we go to sleep right away

But not very often

Sometimes Weenie and Skipperdee and me we get out of bed and go
into that closet and look around for a while and when we get in there
there is this cave and it is so dark in there that it's absolutely black
and there is this big bug in there that has those enormously large
feathers and he picks us up by our necks and sklanks us around in his
paws and carries us down into this deep well that is all filled with
tigers and lions and birds of prey and they eat us up raw and step
on us and stamp their feet on us and absolutely rank us

and we have to run for our lives and drag each other on our stomach
and scrape our face along the side until we are absolutely breathing
and stretching our arms to reach that closet door barely in time
and our heart is beating and we have to wake Nanny with a flashlight
in her face to save us and put witch hazel and cotton on all of our
toenails

And Nanny has to get up and pamper me and spoil me for a while

while I am out of my head with fever and pain

After all I am only 6

Oh my Lord

There's so much to do

Tomorrow I think I'll pour a pitcher of water down the mail chute

Oooooooooooooooooooo I absolutely love The Plaza

THE

ABSOLUTELY ESSENTIAL

ELOISE

SCRAP BOOK

with some rawther interesting material

and colorful comments

 by

ME, ELOISE

The STORY of ELOISE As told by MARIE BRENNER

Kay Thompson and Hilary Knight at the Palm Court of the Plaza Hotel, 1955.

loise gave me permission to rebel. She was a feisty princess of the city, a six-year-old merry prankster in a puffed-sleeved blouse. "I am Eloise! I am six!" she exclaimed with brio in 1955, and it was like a clarion call, a preview of the 1960s sensibility. It felt as if Eloise were America's first little naughty girl. I saw myself in the mirror she held up, and to this day I cannot pass a mailbox without a desire to douse it with a pitcher of water. Eloise was our ticket out of a gray flannel society—Holden Caulfield for kindergarten girls. We marveled at her exotic life at the Plaza Hotel and bombarded our mothers with questions: Where were Eloise's parents? How come she was so lucky to stay home from school? We wanted her life. This pint-sized creature of Manhattan society heralded the coming arrival of a Day-Glo world.

Eloise hit at a moment when class and status were changing quickly. She was an altogether thrilling new heroine, an antidote to Heidi the drip, and the peppy, but sappy Nancy Drew. Unlike Dick and Jane, Eloise would never hop, skip, or jump. She lived mother-free in a poor-little-rich-girl paradise without rules. As she raced from a mint raid in the Empire Room to spy from the Baroque ceiling of the Grand Ballroom, she lured us into an intoxicating urban fantasy. Her Plaza was as magical as Oz, as exotic as *South Pacific*. She could sklonk the kneecaps of Vincent the barber as deftly as she could order up *petit déjeuner* or "Planked Medallion of Beef Tenderloin with Fresh Vegetables Maison . . . and two raisins, one strawberry leaf and one clams in season."

For Eden Ross Lipson, the children's book editor of *The New York Times,* "Eloise defines New York in the way that Madeline defines Paris." Eloise was alone but cosseted in luxury. Her toys were two broken dolls, Sabine and Saylor, but then she had access to the unimaginable—the hotel fire hose and thermostats. There was also a touch of Cinderella in her story: Her friends were Johanna, the maid; the elevator operator; and the churlish manager, Mr. Salomone.

Eloise appeared to improvise her world as she went along: She skibbled and skiddered down the hall, spoke on a paper cup telephone to Mars, and sklathed herself on pillows at night. Her nightmares featured big bugs with feathers that sklanked her around in their paws, but she was inevitably saved by Nanny, who put witch hazel on all of her toenails. On Christmas Eve, orphaned in the vast splendor of the Plaza with Nanny and her turtle, Skipperdee, and her pug, Weenie, Eloise dreamed of zimbering reindeer in Central Park.

ay Thompson's *Eloise: A Book for Precocious Grownups* was first launched in 1955, in the chill of the Cold War. The illustrator Hilary Knight's striking palette—black and white and pink and red—exploded off the pages like a geyser and cascaded into our houses, inspiring us with the idea of our own possibilities. It was clear in the drawings and in her words: Eloise was a mini-Auntie Mame, a protofeminist. Like her creator, Kay Thompson, Eloise was independent and saucy. She was an ancient child with the musical vocabulary of a poet. Her words would enter the language of Eisenhower's America.

The book was an immediate sensation, which startled the author. "I am the last person—the really truly last person—who would ever write a children's book," she said in an interview. In New York, editor Jack Goodman, who also edited S. J. Perelman and Irwin Shaw, issued a memo dated November 18, 1955: "Thursday evening first copies came off press. Friday morning at 9:30 people in the office who had taken home copies came in making considerable noise. Friday morning at 11:30 we ordered a second printing. Friday afternoon, *Life* magazine told us they are running a story on *Eloise* (pictures and text in two colors) in their December 5th issue." Soon the book was selling four thousand copies a week; it shared the bestseller list that April with John O'Hara's *Ten North Frederick* and Graham Greene's *The Quiet American*.

I joined a long line of thousands of little girls who felt, as I did, that Eloise had sent a spear directly into our own hearts. I saw who I was in her, and she helped define my place in the world. The Inner Eloise Club has many distinguished members. "She was my way out of Brooklyn into Manhattan," the playwright Wendy Wasserstein said of her in the autumn of 1998. The writer Delia Ephron recalled cel-

Me in an ad for the Plaza with enormously attractive prices, 1956.

ebrating Eloise's sensibility in her own children's book: *How to Eat Like a Child.*

Marooned in the suburbs, we were Brownies and watched black-and-white TV. Our parents drove station wagons, had picture windows, and read *Marjorie Morningstar*. Hems were below the knee, Shirley Jones was in *Carousel* and women's magazines featured recipes for tuna casserole made with potato chips and cream of mushroom soup. Eloise invited us to *terra incognita*, a life outside Kansas. The flap copy announced her milieu: She was "not yet pretty" but "already a Person" whom Henry James, whoever he was, would want to study, and Queen Victoria and the New York Jets would want to adopt. Her Plaza was rich and protected; it stood on Fifth Avenue. Eloise's absent ghost-mother went to Gstaad, charged at Bergdorf's, and talked to her stockbroker.

The 1950s were Eloise's period, and she helped to define them. *Eloise* was more than a popular book; the dolls, toys, and wardrobe it generated constituted one of publishing's first saturation-marketing gambits. There was even a special room at the Plaza where one could pick up a telephone and hear the voice of Eloise, high-pitched and childlike. The voice was, actually, that of Kay Thompson. *"Hello, it's me, Eloise."* By 1963, more than a million copies of

Eloise and its sequels had been sold. At the height of the craze, Thompson staged tea parties at the Plaza at which she would vamp as Eloise, and helped mastermind a Plaza menu for children with "Teeny Weenies" and "Eggs Eloise" on it. Thompson traveled to Dallas to launch Eloise clothing at Neiman Marcus, and Eloise dolls were sold at Lord & Taylor.

Eloise was free to express the dark gleams of her inside. She could offer rubber candy to adults and let fly with her opinions. My daughter, Casey, on discovering Eloise when she was six, said of her reverentially: "She is a bad girl!" Thumbing through my own tattered copy all these years later, I see that I scrawled my name messily in crayon on most of the pages. Eloise was not allowed to belong to anybody else. I truly believed that I owned her.

(above) Good Housekeeping *featured clothing from the Neiman Marcus Eloise collection in 1958.*
(above right) Kay in 1934, when she and her sisters were appearing with bandleader Fred Waring.

Very little is known of Kay Thompson's early life. A biographical note gives her birth date as November 9, 1909. She was born in St. Louis and named Katherine Fink. Later, she changed her name to the more euphonious Thompson, but her family always referred to her as Kitty. She

attended the same high school as Tennessee Williams, and went to Washington University. Thompson's father, a jeweler, encouraged his daughter's musical ability. By the time she was sixteen, she was a prodigy on the piano, performing Liszt with the St. Louis Symphony. She remained close to her two sisters, but she rarely talked about her childhood with friends.

THE FILMS of KAY THOMPSON

FUNNY FACE

s a young woman Thompson had an ebullience in her face, with a lightness around the edges. She was tall and skinny, with red hair, strong sharp features and extraordinary agate eyes. She was handsome and offbeat and possessed a kind of mannish look that was not in vogue at the time. She became notorious for trademark trailing scarves, and toreador pants. "She could take ten yards of black jersey and make it look like a Schiaparelli," the film critic Rex Reed said of her.

Like Eloise, Kay Thompson seemed to exist center stage, with her family off in the wings. As a young woman, it was her ambition to be a musical star, but she was twenty years ahead of her time, a gifted oddball before high camp was chic. In 1937 Kay was cast in a Shubert production called *Hooray for What!* Her rehearsal pianist was Hugh Martin, who went on to write with Ralph Blane the haunting score for *Meet Me in St. Louis*. Before Martin went off to war, he told MGM to hire Thompson. He later said, "She was to vocal arrangements what Louis Armstrong was to jazz."

In the history of popular American music, Kay Thompson's role has been largely unreported. At Metro, she was part of a hallowed

(top) Kay with her first husband, jazz trombonist Jack Jenny, in Kay's first film, Manhattan Merry-Go-Round, *1938.*

Judy Garland and Liza Minnelli, 1949. Many people say Liza was the model for me Eloise. When asked, Kay said, "Eloise is all me."

concentration of talent run by Arthur Freed, the producer of *Singin' in the Rain, An American in Paris,* and *Gigi.* Her vocal arrangements helped bring jazz rhythms to MGM musicals, and she worked with the best of the studio's talent. She is credited with teaching Lena Horne to sing loud and with giving Judy Garland an entirely new sound. Lena Horne told me, "Kay was a major part of my time at MGM. Professionally, she developed me as a singer completely. I had the groundwork there, but I did not know how to get it out. She was the best vocal coach in the world."

Thompson and Garland developed such a close friendship that Thompson was the godmother of Garland's daughter, Liza Minnelli, who took care of Kay in later life. When Thompson met Garland, the singer was still a beloved ingenue, fixed in the public imagination with Mickey Rooney, a perpetual Dorothy singing "Over the Rainbow." Thompson honed in on her vulnerability and brought out her mature feelings; she gave her sophistication. Kay Thompson is credited with putting the sob in Garland's voice and softening her tone. Thompson's own style was like a shadow print behind each Garland performance. There was the hand on the hip—a gesture Liza Minnelli later adopted as well— and a very distinct bow with one arm perpendicular and the other behind her back.

By the end of Thompson's time at Metro, her style was easily recognizable; you could tell which singers had been trained by her.

(left) The Freed Unit at MGM, in conference for the 1946 film Till the Clouds Roll By. Counterclockwise from left: Kay; conductor/arranger Lennie Hayton; choreographer Robert Alton; actress Lucille Bremer; producer Arthur Freed; composer Jerome Kern. (below) Lena Horne, singing "Bill," a number cut from Till the Clouds Roll By.

(below counterclockwise from right) Kay, MGM music director Roger Edens, film director Vincente Minnelli, and actress Greer Garson. Kay and Edens created a musical number for Garson to perform in MGM's Ziegfeld Follies (1946).

In this drawing by Hilary Knight, they are previewing the number, a parody called "Madame Crematon," for Garson, who was not amused. The show-stopping role went to Judy Garland (above), and under Kay's direction, Garland acquired a totally new image.

KAY'S CLUB ACT

However, she became increasingly restless at MGM, and her marriage to CBS Radio producer Bill Spier was close to divorce. So Thompson came up with a daring plan to reinvent her life by taking center stage in a nightclub with a singing group of four young brothers behind her.

Thompson, who could always spot talent, discovered Andy Williams and his three siblings to complete her act. Williams was then in his early twenties and already at Metro, years away from his signature hit "Moon River." Thompson created an entirely new way to entertain an audience. "Now we are used to seeing a girl with four or eight guys, but at that time vocal groups had never done anything but stand around the microphone at the end of a number and put their arms up. It was that static!" Williams later said. "We acted out scenes like a miniature Broadway show. When we got on the stage at El Rancho Vegas, we realized that no one could hear us. We hung microphones from a beam across the stage—this had never been done before."

She irreverently referred to her new career as "the saloon beat." When she opened in Las Vegas, the act was paid $2,500 a week, at a time when Sophie Tucker was making $5,000. Eight weeks later, Thompson and the Williams brothers moved to Ciro's in Los Angeles. "Walter Winchell began writing about us. Within a year we were making $15,000 a week," Williams said.

(left) Don Freeman's lithograph of Kay, with a nod toward Toulouse-Lautrec. (below) Kay in performance with the Williams Brothers.

Andy is second from right.

When they opened at Le Directoire in New York in April 1948, *Variety* ran the headline: KAY THOMPSON'S NEW CAFE WOW and praised her as "an atomic bomb of rhythm songapation."

loise began as a vocal riff, a droll bit of shtick to pass the time between friends. Thompson once recalled she was late for a photo session at the California home of Robert Alton, MGM's dance coach. "I drove the car across a golf course—Bob's house was right there. I got out of the car and I went a few steps. And he said, 'Who do you think you are, coming here five minutes late?' I said, 'I am Eloise, I am six.'

"From that moment on, while we were rehearsing, everybody became somebody else. When we ran into each other, there were all these crazy voices going. People wanted to know just about everything about Eloise, and I would make up these terrible outrageous things. When we were on the road, Eloise came when we needed her. We would get to the train and somebody would say, 'Who's got the tickets?' Bob would say, 'Ask Eloise.' Suddenly, I was thrust into the role."

During her last years, Kay Thompson told the writer Stephen Silverman, "I think the story of our lives comes from these wonderful people we run into. You meet a stranger and, 'My God, the electricity!'" Such luck and happy coincidence were at the very center of the history of *Eloise*. By the early 1950s, Thompson had become a fixture of the Persian Room at the Plaza, and she lived rent-free in the hotel. One of her close friends was a young fashion editor at *Harper's Bazaar*, D. D. Dixon. A style-setter in Manhattan during the golden postwar years, Dixon would later appear on the International Best Dressed list as D. D. Ryan, the wife of the financier John Ryan, but even as a young woman she had immense flair. More than that, she had a gift for seeing the shock of the new, and she was intrigued not only by Kay Thompson but also by the work of a young illustrator named Hilary Knight who, as it happened, was her neighbor in a brownstone on West 52nd Street.

(above) Kay and Hilary working on a new project — an unpublished magazine piece called "Eloise in Hollywood" — in Kay's dressing room on the set of Funny Face.

According to Ryan,

"Kay would call me and do Eloise on the phone. She would say 'This is Eloise' in that funny little voice. I finally said, 'Kay, you really ought to write this down!' I said, 'There is a fellow across the hall, a great friend of mine, Hilary Knight.' He used to make little drawings and shove them under my door. One morning he made a drawing of two little girls, one a fat little pretty prissy girl with frizzy blond corkscrews. The other was the complete opposite, and that feisty little girl made me think of Kay's Eloise voice. I told Kay, 'I have a drawing of Eloise.' And Kay got enormously interested."

Kay posing with Evelyn Rudie, who played me in the 1956 Eloise *television special.*

In the history of artistic collaboration, Kay Thompson and Hilary Knight would become as fused as Lewis Carroll and John Tenniel. As with Tenniel's drawings of Alice, it is impossible to imagine Eloise any other way than as she was first pictured by Knight. Knight, a soft-spoken native New Yorker, had been a student of the painter Reginald Marsh. He was twenty-seven in 1954 when he was introduced to Thompson, and in the beginning stages of his career as a magazine illustrator.

Knight recalled, "I just *knew* this little girl Eloise. D. D. took me to meet Kay—I believe it was her last performance at the Persian Room. We went to the lobby, and I remember sitting with her, and she told me about the book. We started working on it right away." Thompson would remember writing "twelve lines on a piece of paper, turning to Hilary, and saying, 'If you are interested, get in touch with me.' Then I spoke a few words of Eloisiana and left."

That Christmas, Thompson received a card from Knight, a drawing of an angel and Santa Claus streaking through the sky. On top of Santa's pack was Eloise. Thompson was elated. "There she was in person. I knew at once Hilary Knight had to illustrate the book . . . I holed in at the Plaza and we went to work. I just knew I had to get this done. Eloise was trying to get out. I've never known such stimulation. This girl had complete control of me. Ideas came from everywhere. Hilary and I had an immediate understanding. We wrote, edited, laughed, outlined, cut, pasted, laughed again, read out loud, laughed and suddenly we had a book."

There was an ingenious quality to Knight's drawings, an economy of line—almost as if they were preliminary sketches. He had a perfect eye for class differences, balancing hotel guests and maids, and he filled the page with drawings, rather than following the traditional one-picture-to-a-page storytelling technique.

Knight told me that he believed his artist parents inspired his drawing style.

"But if D. D. had not come along, this would have never happened. It was just a game that Kay did with her friends. She would have gotten bored with it and forgotten it. D. D. is so important in this. She made it possible for *Eloise* to be born."

HILARY'S FAMILY TREE

THE STORY OF HILARY KNIGHT

An evolution in his own words and pictures

This is my story of how the visual Eloise evolved.

I was born on November 1, 1926, in New York, and grew up with my parents and older brother, Joey. Our house was an 1845 farmhouse in historic Roslyn, Long Island.

My father and mother, Clayton Knight and Katharine Sturges, were artist-writers in an era ripe with new ideas and incredible style—the 1920s and '30s.

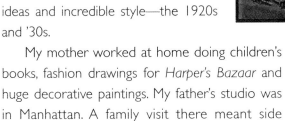

My mother worked at home doing children's books, fashion drawings for *Harper's Bazaar* and huge decorative paintings. My father's studio was in Manhattan. A family visit there meant side trips to theaters, museums, and, as a special treat, tea in the Plaza Hotel's Palm Court.

Often my parents worked together. A 1926 *New Yorker* cover designed by my mother was executed as a woodcut by my father. Its pink, black, and white colors were echoed in *Eloise* years later.

Individually, my parents illustrated landmark books. My father's experiences as a World War I ace led in 1929 to *Pilots' Luck*.

My mother's trip to Asia in 1917 inspired the drawings for *Little Pictures of Japan* (1925). Her 1930 painting of a sassy child whose stance, attitude, and color palette remained in my subconscious throughout my early life powerfully contributed to the final vision of Eloise.

Evo•lu•tion: The theory that various types of animals and plants (and six-year-olds) have developed from previously existing kinds.

My Roslyn bedroom with murals
painted by my mother.

1 On my bedroom shelf were books with illustrations that helped form the basis of my style, from the delicate penline of Ernest Shepard's 1931 *Wind in the Willows* to Edmund Dulac's exotic fantasies. But it was Maurice Boulet De Monvel's 1887 book of manners *La Civilité* that was my particular favorite. His drawings of naughty children using damask curtains for handkerchiefs and forks as combs planted the seed that became Eloise.

2 My family's move to New York City was a new adventure. Less thrilling for me was schooling: City and Country School and Friends Seminary were an endurance test. Before I joined the navy I spent a year at the Art Students' League. It changed my life.

3 After World War II, I returned to the League to study with Reginald Marsh, a brilliant artist and teacher. What he taught me about anatomy I later used to animate Eloise.

4 By 1948 I had my own studio and a very special neighbor, D. D. Dixon. It was an exciting time for me: designing greeting cards, murals, and illustrations for magazines, such as *Mademoiselle* and *House and Garden*.

5 This is an unpublished drawing of two little girls. The prissy one Kay would call Dorothy Darling. The other suggested the wicked schoolgirls of Ronald Searle. They combined to become the visual Eloise.

6 Kay Thompson, after our Plaza Hotel meeting, wrote a dazzling outline for Eloise and I began to draw.

7 This 1954 Christmas card from me to Kay was the first picture of Eloise fully evolved. It led to a year of intense and exhilarating collaboration.

8 And in November 1955, *Eloise* was born.

9 I made a painting of Eloise as a birthday gift for Kay on November 9, 1956 (she was a Scorpio, as are Eloise and I). Kay in turn gave it to the Plaza. A few years later it vanished. (The mystery is still unsolved, though Kay blamed rowdy debutantes.) I replaced it with a new oil portrait in 1964, where it has remained a magnet for Eloise admirers over the years . . .

10 . . . among whom were my nephew Christopher Knight and his twin sisters, Kitty and Lily (more Scorpios), models for later editions of Eloise.

11 *Eloise*, a Thanksgiving television special that aired in 1957, did not please Kay, and soon dropped from sight.

12 An early version of Weenie, the dog who looks like a cat. Weenie later became a pug, because pugs and Siamese cats have the same coloring. When the Duke and Duchess of Windsor adopted the breed as their official pets, Kay and I knew we had made the right choice.

13 This apple represents the three sequels to Eloise. They too have been out of sight—till now.

14 In November 1997 the Museum of the City of New York (which I visited as a child) installed a corner of Eloise's room in their permanent toy gallery.

15 In today's disposable world it is remarkable how many things in my life have remained the same. I can revisit: the Roslyn house; our apartment building at 43 Fifth Avenue; my father's studio in the Beaux Arts Building on East 44th Street; and the schools I attended. All are virtually unchanged. And Eloise, incredibly, will remain six years old forever.

A black leather scrapbook rests on a shelf in Hilary Knight's apartment on East 51st Street in New York. In it is the entire history of the phenomenon that *Eloise* became. Eloise mimics appeared in the columns, and Eloise mannequins gamboled in the Christmas windows of Bergdorf Goodman; caricatures of Thompson and Knight and their six-year-old vixen cropped up frequently in the papers. At Simon & Schuster, Richard Grossman worked on the original promotion campaign with Jack Goodman. Later, he would edit Kay Thompson and become a close friend. "Kay had a clear idea of what she wanted—to get out of the 'saloon business.'" So Grossman and Goodman quickly rounded up a roster of glossy personalities to "blurb" the book. "To me *Eloise* is the most glorious book ever written about an endearingly frightful little girl. Completely enchanting, and you can quote me fulsomely," Cornelia Otis Skinner said of it. Noel Coward's appraisal was printed in the ads: "Frankly, I adore Eloise."

The book's success did not eclipse Thompson's Hollywood reputation. In 1956, she was asked to play a supporting role in *Funny Face* as the redoubtable Maggie Prescott, who storms her way to Europe and lands in France singing the enduring "Bonjour, Paris!" "I never considered anyone else for the part," director Stanley Donen told his biographer Stephen Silverman. Thompson's image was italicized by her staccato interpretation of a fashion editor

inspired by Diana Vreeland of *Vogue*. Like Vreeland, Thompson was brassy and shrewd. "She's got to have bizzazz!" she declaimed about one model, and the newly coined word soon found its way into fashion copy. For the rest of her life, she would often end conversations with a vibrant "Think pink!" "Think Pink!" was the remarkable opening musical number in *Funny Face*, in which Thompson instructed her staff at *Quality* magazine to "banish the black, bury the blue, burn the beige. Think pink! And that includes the kitchen sink!"

Soon, Thompson and Hilary Knight went to work on a sequel, *Eloise in Paris*. Kay was determined to put Eloise in a small Left Bank

(above) The jacket for Eloise in Paris. *(right) An early version of the* Paris *jacket.*

hotel, the Relais Bisson. She and Knight set off to Paris to research the book, and Knight walked the city sketching scenery—the Pont Neuf, Sacré Coeur.

Simon & Schuster planned a record ad campaign for *Eloise in Paris*. Kay was photographed with Dean Acheson at book-and-author lunches; Eloise endorsed Renaults and Kalistron luggage.

(left) In Paris, 1956, a dress design for Eloise was dictated by Christian Dior to his young assistant, Yves Saint Laurent, who drew this sketch.

(above right) How Dior and YSL appeared in Eloise in Paris. *(below right) An unpublished drawing by Hilary Knight, 1956.*

This is how Hilary thought I would have looked in Dior.

In 1957, Thompson and Knight followed their editor Robert Bernstein to Random House. There, they quickly produced the immensely popular *Eloise at Christmastime*, with sales in the hundreds of thousands.

After *Christmastime* was published, Richard Grossman had an idea. "Russia was in the news. There was so much talk about *Sputnik* and Krushchev, and I thought, Kay belongs in Moscow with Hilary! I thought it would be amusing for Eloise to be there." In Moscow, Thompson and Knight set up at the National Hotel. Many nights they went to the Bolshoi, Knight later recalled. Thompson wore three cashmere sweaters, special wool fezzes, and a red coat made of guanaco, a thick camel-like fur. Thompson returned, Grossman later remembered, with "a real sense of paranoia" about the Russia she encountered, and *Eloise in Moscow*, published in 1959, has the satirical darkness of a spy story. Eloise peeks through grilles and under doors; she cries at a performance of *Anna Karenina* and takes a bath in a raccoon hat. She says *"pajalasta"* and *"spasobo"*—please and thank-you—to a dazed Russian room-service clerk, and samples black caviar from the Caspian Sea. Knight's exquisitely detailed color foldout of the Kremlin is the centerpiece of the book. At a time when the Cold War still terrified America's schoolchildren, *Eloise in Moscow* opened a window into a shuttered civilization.

In the summer of 1966, Hilary Knight went to Rome to work with Kay Thompson on their fifth collaboration. At the height of her celebrity, in 1962, Thompson had moved from New York and taken a splendid maisonette at the top of the Palazzo Torlonia, near the

(top) *The jacket for* Eloise at Christmastime. (middle) *The jacket for* Eloise in Moscow.

This is how I might have appeared on the jacket of Eloise Takes a Bawth.

Spanish Steps. From her terrace she could see the Baroque domes of the city. Her rooms were as fantastic as ever. The furniture consisted of zebra-skin rugs and tables she had painted with red lacquer nail polish. While in Rome, she worked on a book called *The Fox and the Fig* with the young playwright Mart Crowley, who would later write the seminal play about gay life, *The Boys in the Band*. Though Crowley and Kay worked extensively on it, *The Fox and the Fig* never went to press.

Also in Rome, Knight had drawn hundreds of sketches for a new idea: *Eloise Takes a Bawth*. There was Eloise lolling in an overflowing bathtub deluging movie stars in fox coats and the Plaza's long-suffering manager, Mr. Salomone, but Thompson and Knight could not resolve the story. Just as *Eloise Takes a Bawth* was ready to go to press, Thompson pulled it from the publisher. Later she refused to allow *Eloise in Paris*, *Eloise in Moscow*, and *Eloise at Christmastime* to remain in print.

Thompson remained active in a number of creative projects, including a hugely successful fashion show in Versailles in 1968. But she never returned to Eloise.

In the last years of Thompson's life, I spent months trying to interview her. She would not allow it, but she did call me on the telephone on several occasions, her voice brimming with theatrical enthusiasm. She would not identify herself when she called; she felt there was no need. "I do not want my story to be told. I am too busy working. But do call again. Maybe someday I will talk." She never did.

Kay Thompson died peacefully in New York on July 6, 1998, at the East Side apartment of her goddaughter, Liza Minnelli.

(above left) Kay in her last film, Tell Me that You Love Me, Junie Moon, *1970*.
(above right) A recent photo of Hilary in his Manhattan studio.

MY PORTRAIT

T hey still come to see Eloise. They skibble and skidder through the gold lobby where the azaleas bloom in November in the Plaza's Palm Court. The little children and their mothers stand and look up dreamily at Eloise's whimsical portrait.

On a chilly night in November 1998, I too stood out on the corner of 59th Street and Fifth Avenue, looking at Eloise's home, a hotel I had first made my mother take me to in 1957 so that I could pick up the house phone and hear *"Hello, it's me, Eloise."* More than forty years later, I could feel my mother's hand holding mine on that windy corner. I heard voices coming from the red carpeted steps. It was a young mother and her daughters, the tourists like my mother and I had once been, and the woman held a New York City map in her hand. "It's the Plaza Hotel, where Eloise lived!" she exclaimed, and the little girls shrieked with delight. As I watched them disappear into the hotel in search of a six-year-old in a black pleated skirt, I noticed a shiny new brass plaque on the wall.

The famous picture of me at the Plaza.

LITERARY LANDMARKS REGISTER

THE PLAZA HOTEL

THE HOME OF ELOISE

KAY THOMPSON LIVED AT THE PLAZA WHILE WRITING *ELOISE*, FIRST PUBLISHED IN 1955. MISS THOMPSON AND ILLUSTRATOR HILARY KNIGHT BROUGHT THIS FICTITIOUS CHARMER TO LIFE; AN EXUBERANT AND PRECOCIOUS SIX-YEAR-OLD WHO LIVED ON THE TOP FLOOR OF THE HOTEL.

DESIGNATED A LITERARY LANDMARK, SEPTEMBER 26, 1998